Read & Feel™
PUBLISHING

ISBN 979-8-9856727-2-5

Published by Read & Feel Publishing
Brooklyn, New York
(646) 980-0471

ifyourbestfriend.com
readandfeel.us

Printed in China

An elf's name may seem strange,
And clearly out of range.

But when an elf is your best friend,
You get to change its NAME!

To visit the **Elf Village**,
You can't be very tall.

You need a little elf magic,
To make you very small.

As you journey to Elf Village,
Flowers look like trees.

Giant bees come racing past,
Elf magic makes you *BREEZE!*

Elf Village is amazing,
It's colorful and dandy.

When you take a deep breath in,
You smell your favorite **candy!**

You only knew about your friend,
And you are happy to no end.

But as your elf friend shows you around,
Six talented Elves can now be found.

Then Jiggy the DANCING elf,
Gives you elves' shoes to wear.

Toot plays a **Tune** with his flute,
To relax you so you've not a care.

Toy making elves are full of cheer,
They make gifts that are *FUN.*

But then they get a call from Santa.
"It's Christmas eve, You have to run."

When you come out the other end...

YOU ARE AT THE NORTH POLE!!!

Everything is *GO, GO, GO,*
Getting ready for Santa's flight.

Then your best friend asks a magical question,

And so you fly with Santa,
Your best friend by your side,
Delivering presents around the world,

On a magical Christmas ride.

When you get back to the North Pole,
You're happy and hungry too.

You're greeted with an amazing feast,
For Santa, the elves... and YOU!

It's time for you to go home.
A magical *HOLE* appears.

You jump into it but before you're gone,
The elves give you three cheers!

As you remember your adventures
You happily close your eyes.

By the time your head hits the pillow,
You return to your very own size.

Then your best friend transforms to a doll
For a final elf magic SURPRISE.

Find more best friends
With the continuing Book Series.

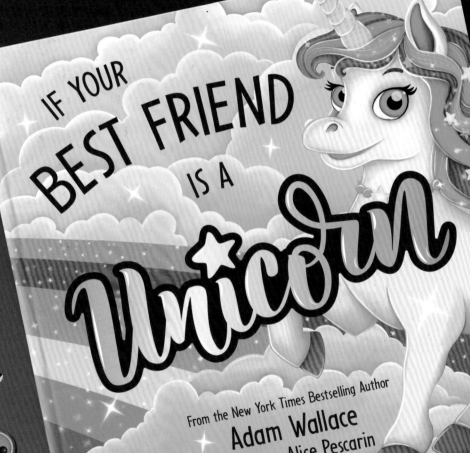

IF YOUR
BEST FRIEND
IS A
Unicorn

From the New York Times Bestselling Author
Adam Wallace
Illustrated by Alice Pescarin